Everything's ROSIE

The Special Invitation

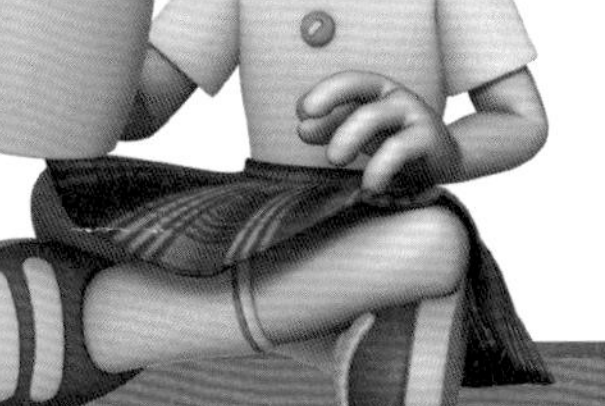

EGMONT
We bring stories to life

When you see these symbols:

Read aloud
Read aloud to your child.

Read alone
Support your child as they read alone.

Read along
Read along with your child.

Egmont is passionate about helping to preserve the world's remaining ancient forests. We only use paper from legal and sustainable forest sources.

This book is made from paper certified by the Forestry Stewardship Council® (FSC®), an organisation dedicated to promoting responsible management of forest resources. For more information on the FSC®, please visit www.fsc.org. To learn more about Egmont's sustainable paper policy, please visit www.egmont.co.uk/ethical

Rosie and Raggles had spent all morning playing with the dressing-up box, but now it was time to tidy up.

"I think that's everything, Raggles," said Rosie, dropping the final shoe into the box.

"Oh good," said Raggles, and he let out a large yawn. "Now for some serious hammock time!"

But just as Raggles bounced into his hammock for a rest, there was a rat-a-tat-tat at the door. Rosie and Raggles had a visitor!

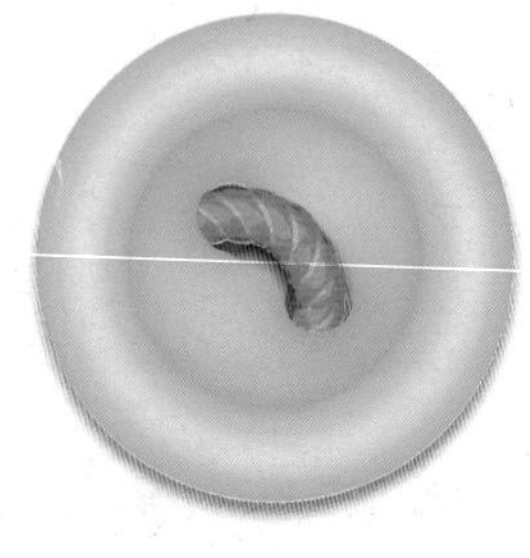

Read alone

Rosie and Raggles are tidying up the Playhouse. There is a knock on the door.

Rosie opened the door to find Big Bear standing outside, looking confused. "Come in, Big Bear," smiled Rosie. "What's the matter?'

Big Bear squeezed through the doorway. "It's this," said Big Bear, and he read aloud from a piece of card: "Dear Big Bear, please can you come to my palace for tea? From the Queen."

"But why are you frowning?" Rosie asked Big Bear. "You're going to have tea with the Queen!"

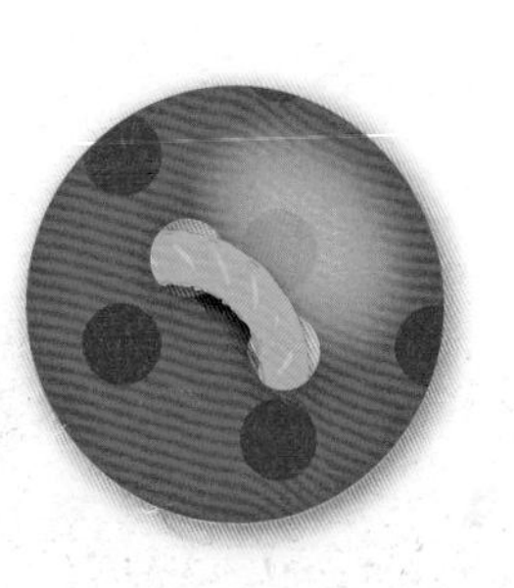

Read alone

Big Bear has an invitation to meet the Queen!
Rosie and Raggles are very excited for him.

"I'm worried," Big Bear sighed. "I've never had tea with the Queen before! What if I get crumbs on my whiskers? Or jelly on my paws?"

"Well, luckily you've come to the right place," giggled Rosie. "Raggles and I will teach you how to have tea with a queen."

A grin spread across Big Bear's face. "Oh, thank you both!" he beamed.

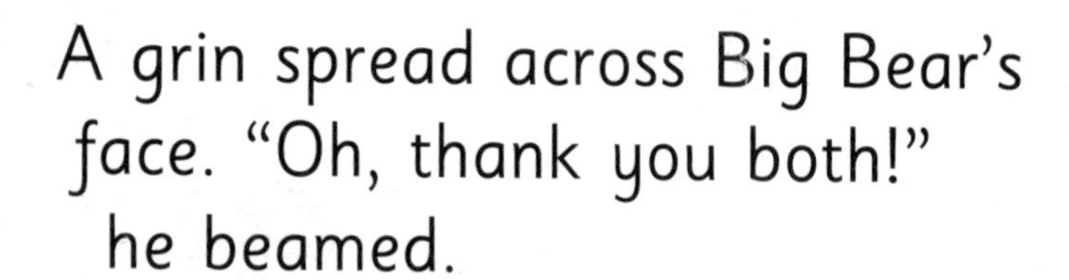

Big Bear has never had tea with a queen.
Rosie offers to help him get ready.

"First," Rosie told Big Bear kindly, "you have to dress right."

They all looked through the dressing-up box, and pulled out a pink cape, an orange top hat and a pair of purple ear-warmers. Big Bear tried each of them on, but he didn't like any of them.

Rosie thought for a moment, then she had an idea. "Wait there!" she called as she dashed away. She came back holding a small red bow tie and gently put it on Big Bear.

"Perfect!" said Raggles.

Rosie and Raggles help Big Bear find smart clothes. They choose a red bow tie.

"Next," said Raggles, "you have to walk tall, with confidence!"

"Easy peasy," said Big Bear and he did his best walk. But he still walked like a bear.

"We'll get you walking like a prince," said Rosie. She gently placed a book on top of his head to help him stand up straight. "Now try to walk up Oakley's Hill."

And off Big Bear went, trying as hard as he could not to drop the book. He felt very silly, but Raggles cheered him on.

Read alone

Next they help Big Bear walk tall.
He feels very silly.

At the same time, Will was hiding in a flower bed, watching as Big Bear struggled to balance the book on his head.

"This is my best trick ever! Big Bear having tea with the Queen," he snorted. "As if!"

As he watched Big Bear, Will's eyes fell on Holly, who was in the playground.

"I wonder if Holly would like to go to tea with the Queen too?" Will sniggered to himself. He took a postcard and a pencil out of his pocket and began to write another invitation.

Read alone

Will wrote the invitation as a trick!
He writes another one to Holly.

Up on Oakley's Hill, Rosie, Raggles and Big Bear were practising drinking tea.

"Great slurping!" said Raggles as Big Bear took a really long slurp of his tea.

Big Bear felt very proud of his slurping skills. But there was one last lesson to learn – how to speak clearly.

"Repeat clearly after me," Oakley smiled. "Rosie and Raggles ran around the roundabout." Every word was spoken perfectly! Big Bear took a big breath ...

Oakley tries to teach Big Bear to speak clearly. He teaches him a tongue twister.

"Rosie and Raggles round-a-ran about the run ... oh." He stopped. Rosie and Raggles smiled at him kindly.

Big Bear tried again. "Rosie and roundabout raggled round and ran and about ..." He'd got muddled again!

But Big Bear was determined. He let out a big sigh, took in a big breath and tried one last time. "Rosie and Raggles ran around the roundabout."

He'd done it! He was ready to meet the Queen.

Big Bear says Oakley's tongue twister.
Now he is ready to meet the Queen!

Suddenly, Holly came rushing up Oakley's Hill.

"I've got an invitation!" Holly told them, waving a piece of card in front of her. "It says, 'Dear Holly, please can you come to my palace for tea? From the Queen.'"

Rosie was speechless, but suddenly there was more commotion as Bluebird fell out of Oakley's branches!

"I, Bluebird, have been invited to tea with the Queen!" she announced grandly.

Holly and Bluebird have invitations as well.
They are both very excited.

"Not you as well!" said Raggles, as Rosie gently took Bluebird's invitation from under her wing. It was exactly the same as Big Bear's and Holly's!

"I know this handwriting!" said Rosie.

"I didn't know you knew the Queen, Rosie," said Oakley in a shocked voice.

"I don't," Rosie said. "But I do know who wrote all these invitations. It was Will!"

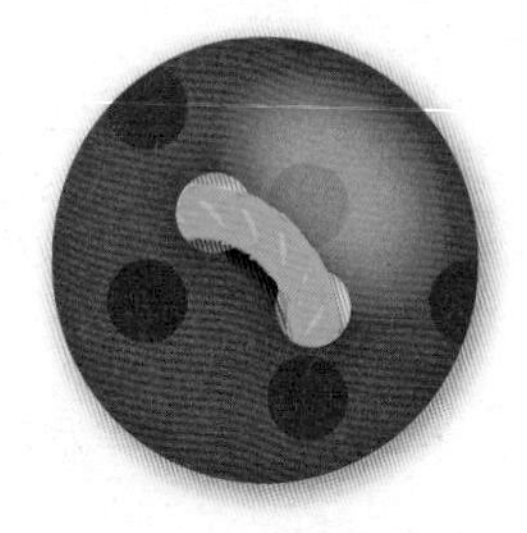

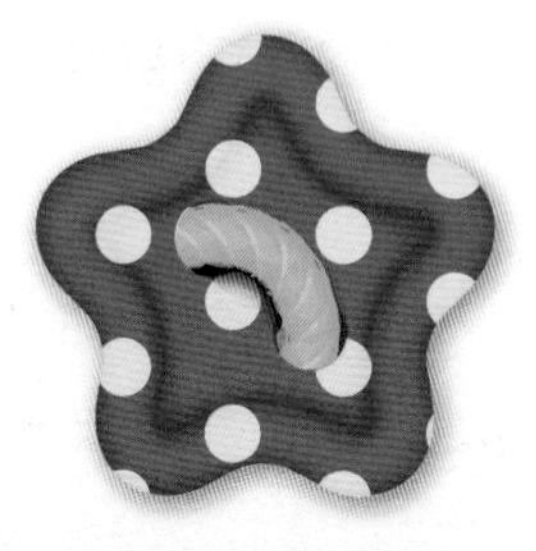

Read alone

Rosie looks at the invitations. She works out it is a trick because she knows Will's writing.

Everyone was very upset.

"But I've had a wash!" cried Big Bear.

"And I've polished my beak!" complained Bluebird grumpily.

Holly said nothing, but her eyes filled with tears. She had been so excited about meeting the Queen, and it was all just a trick.

As Rosie looked at her disappointed friends, an idea popped into her head. "Follow me, everyone!" she smiled. "We're going to have tea with the Queen after all."

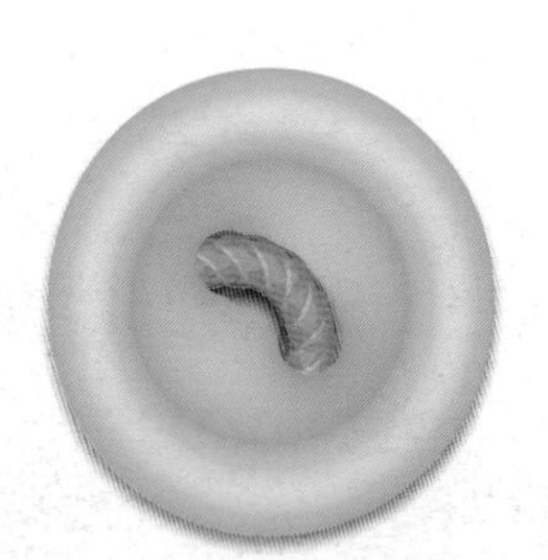

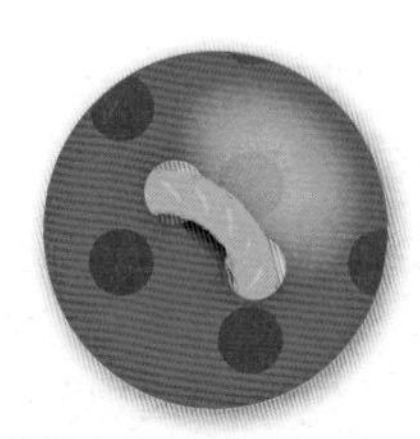

Big Bear, Bluebird and Holly are upset.
But Rosie thinks of a way to meet the Queen.

Meanwhile, Will was still watching his friends, laughing harder than ever. They had all fallen for his trick! But when they all began to walk towards the Playhouse, Will was puzzled. What was going on? He ran ahead of them and sat down on a swing.

"Where are you going?" he asked Big Bear, Holly and Bluebird as they walked past.

"To have tea with the Queen," Holly replied.

"What?" Will said. "It was just a joke!"

Read alone

Will wonders why his friends are still going to tea with the Queen. It had been a trick!

"I can assure you there is nothing funny about tea with Her Majesty," said Bluebird in a posh voice.

"Well, can I come too?" Will asked.

"Have you got an invitation?" Big Bear said.

"No," Will told him.

"Sorry!" came Bluebird's reply, but she didn't sound very sorry at all. As they all walked away towards the Playhouse, Will felt very left out. Maybe his trick wasn't so funny after all, now his friends were having tea without him.

Read alone

Will doesn't have an invitation.
He feels left out.

Back at the Playhouse, Her Royal Highness Rosie and her loyal knight Sir Raggles welcomed their guests to their palace. Rosie wore a shiny crown, and the table was full of cakes and jelly.

Will peered in the window, and decided to ask if he could join in. He knocked on the Playhouse door, and Raggles answered.

"Hello Raggles," said Will quietly. "Can I have tea with you all too?"

"You may," replied Raggles. "But you'll have to be our waiter to make up for tricking Big Bear, Bluebird and Holly."

Rosie dresses up as a queen and everyone has tea. Will asks if he can join in.

Will thought for a moment. "OK," he sighed, and soon he was wearing Rosie's best black jacket and carrying a tray.

Rosie, Raggles, Big Bear, Bluebird and Holly sat around the table and admired how well Big Bear had remembered everything he'd learnt – he sat up straight, slurped his tea and looked very smart in his bow tie. It was just like having tea with the real Queen!

"Except," smiled Rosie, "in this palace you can get jelly on your paws!"

And everyone laughed – even Will!

Will agrees to be the waiter, and everyone enjoys Queen Rosie's tea party!

That night, as they cosied up in their beds, Raggles thought about what life would be like if Rosie was a real queen.

"You could wear the biggest crown ever ... and we could have an ice-cream lake ... and a cake factory!" Raggles beamed at Rosie.

Rosie giggled at her friend getting carried away. "Goodnight, Raggles," she said.

"Goodnight, Rosie," Raggles replied.